Vanishing Colors

Vanishing Colors

Written by Constance Ørbeck-Nilssen

Illustrated by Akin Duzakin

Translated by Kari Dickson

Eerdmans Books for Young Readers

Grand Rapids, Michigan

It is so cold here.
Mama puts her arms around me.
Water runs down the walls,
leaving big puddles on the floor.
We find a spot that is still dry.
I curl up and listen to her voice
as she whispers to me in the dark.

"Tell me about the bird again," I say quietly.
So she tells me about the bird.
The one that swoops down from the mountains as evening falls
and spreads its wings over our house
to protect us from danger.

While we sleep.
While we wait.

I feel the warmth of the bird's feathers.
The warmth of my mother.
I hear her voice, humming softly.
The song about our town.
About all the bridges to places that are now gone.

We wait for the planes that will come.
For the bombs that will fall.
The houses that will collapse around us.
The streets are no longer streets,
just big, deep holes that we cannot cross.
"Soon it will all be over," Mama whispers.
"And everything will be like before."
But how can it be like before?

I listen to her voice until I fall asleep.
When I wake up, she is sleeping.

Can you not sleep?
The huge bird looks at me.
Its eyes shine like beautiful lanterns in the dark.
"No, I dreamed that our house was destroyed," I say. "That we had to leave."
The bird wraps its wings around me.

Have you forgotten everything? it asks.
"What do you mean?" I say.
All the wonderful things that were here before.
I close my eyes.
Try to see everything that was here before.
All the colors.
But I can't see them anymore.
Everything is just dark.

It is early in the morning. The town is still asleep.
The bird looks at me.
You are standing by the window waiting.
Soon the air will be filled with sounds and light.
You are wearing your new dress.

I try to remember. Try to see.
It's as if something grows out of the dark.
"It was red," I say, and smile.

I am waiting for my father.
Soon I will see him, his smiling face,
his open arms.

We walk through the streets.
Papa holds my hand.
Then he stops and points.
Dawn has colored the sky.
We stand quietly and watch
as the colors grow into light.
Then we smile at each other and walk on.

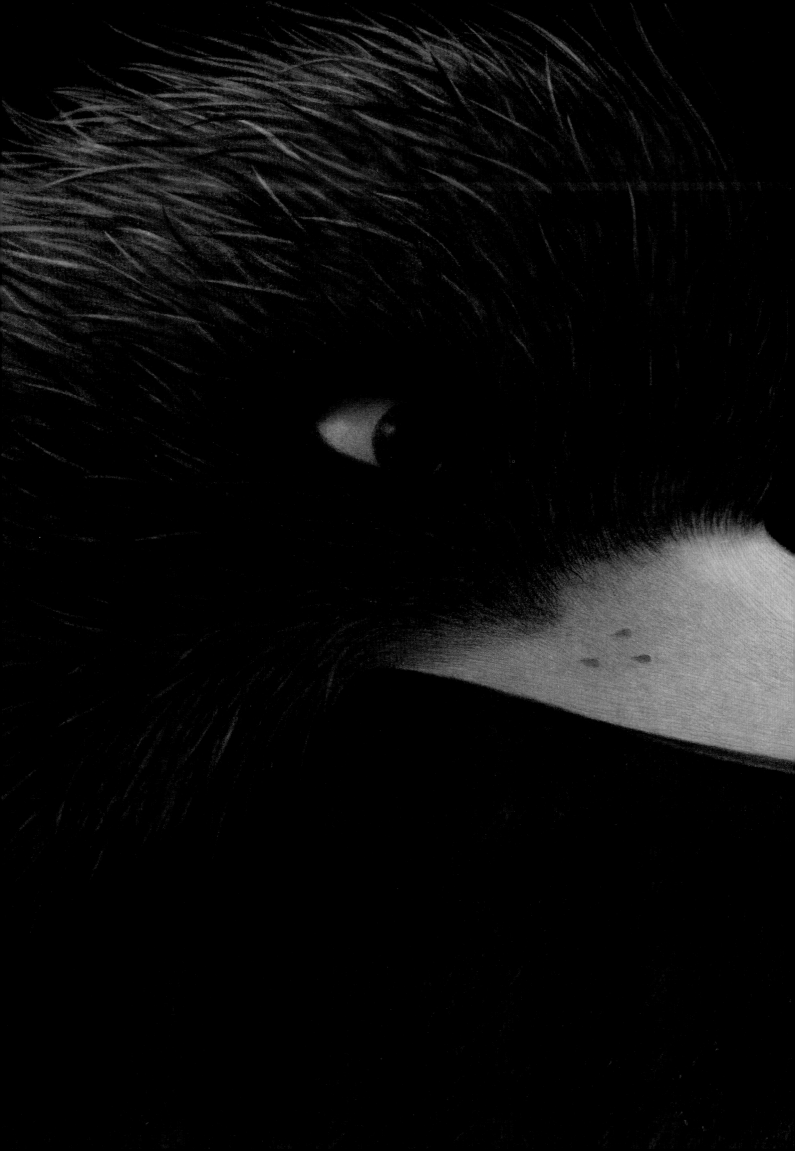

Where are you going? the bird asks.
"We are on our way to the market," I reply.

I try to find something that is hidden deep inside me.
Suddenly, there it is. Like a picture I had lost and now found again.

I see dresses swirling.
Like a thousand suns dancing around me.
Orbiting a planet.
And I am the planet. I spin around and around.

You are carrying a basket, the bird says.
"I am carrying my mother's blankets."
The bird nods.
"I liked the green blanket best," I say.

Soon all the stalls are full of vegetables
and fruit and nuts and flowers.

Do you remember how wonderful it was?
I nod.

*What made you laugh, made your feet dance
and your heart beat faster?* the bird asks.

Where is the music coming from?
It made the whole house shake.
Made the roof open up to the big, blue sky
and the trees bend down to the earth.

"It's Papa who is playing," I whisper.
Yes, the bird says.
The sounds are still there, inside you.

"Are you coming?"

My best friend is standing there waiting for me.
He wants us to be together. All the time.
I wave and shout that I'm coming.
The scent of lilacs fills the air, fills me.

For a moment, I catch a glimpse
of the beautiful bushes
and my friend waiting.
Then the image is gone.

The bird strokes my cheek with its wing.

"You can see further than we can," I say.
"How long can we stay here?"
When you see all the colors in the sky,
you can go, the bird answers.

"But where can we go? All the bridges are gone.
The roads are destroyed. We have no food or water."

The bird lowers its head.
Then folds its wings even tighter around me.
Listen, whispers the bird.

There was once a big flock of birds that set off on a long and dangerous journey.

There were thousands of them.

They had to find somewhere safe where they could all stay.

But they could not agree where to go.

So they decided to ask the oldest bird for advice.

"Stay together," was all the old bird said.

"But Mama and I don't have wings.
How can we cross the river?"

Look up at the rainbow, the bird says.
*It makes a bridge across the sky,
to remind us that there is always a way.
Remember how much more we can do together than alone.*
"But there is only Mama and me," I say.
Stay together, help each other.

The bird lifts its wings and gets ready to take flight.
Then I notice—its wings are no longer simply black.
They are shining.

Mama opens her eyes.
Asks if I have slept a little.
I nod and snuggle in closer.

We wait.
Until the dust has settled.
Until all is quiet again.
Until the big bird
rises up over the mountains
and lets in the morning light.

I take Mama's hand.
We stand for a moment
where there was once a door,
so our eyes can adjust to the light.
I think about Father.
Wonder if I will ever see him again.
I am scared.
But I say nothing.

Then I see the rainbow.
I say all the colors in my head.
Red, orange, yellow, green,
blue, indigo, violet.
I remember everything the bird told me.
And I know that we will find a way.

First published in the United States in 2019 by
Eerdmans Books for Young Readers,
an imprint of Wm. B. Eerdmans Publishing Co.
4035 Park East Court, Grand Rapids, Michigan 49546
www.eerdmans.com/youngreaders

Originally published in Norway in 2017 under the title *Fargene som forsvant* by Vigmostad & Bjørke
Written by Constance Ørbeck-Nilssen • Illustrated by Akin Duzakin
Copyright © Vigmostad & Bjørke, Norway 2017
English-language translation © 2019 Kari Dickson

Manufactured in China

28 27 26 25 24 23 22 21 20 19   1 2 3 4 5 6 7 8 9

ISBN 978-0-8028-5518-3

Library of Congress Cataloging-in-Publication Data

Names: Ørbeck-Nilssen, Constance, 1954- author. | Duzakin, Akin, 1960-
   illustrator.
Title: Vanishing colors / by Constance Ørbeck-Nilssen ; illustrated by Akin
   Duzakin.
Other titles: Fargene som forsvant. English
Description: Grand Rapids, MI : Eerdmans Books for Young Readers, 2019. |
   Summary: "As a young refugee girl takes shelter for the night, the world
   appears bleak. But as she starts thinking about her happy memories, she
   finds the courage to hope for a better future"— Provided by publisher.
Identifiers: LCCN 2018031194 | ISBN 9780802855183 (hardback)
Subjects: | CYAC: Refugees—Fiction. | BISAC: JUVENILE FICTION / Social
   Issues / Emigration & Immigration. | JUVENILE FICTION / Social Issues /
   Homelessness & Poverty. | JUVENILE FICTION / Family / Parents.
Classification: LCC PZ7.O762 Van 2019 | DDC [E]—dc23 LC record available at
   https://lccn.loc.gov/2018031194

This translation has been published with the financial support of NORLA, Norwegian Literature Abroad.

Constance Ørbeck-Nilssen has been writing children's books since 2004. Her previous titles include *Why Am I Here?* and *I'm Right Here* (both Eerdmans), and her books have been published in fifteen countries. She lives in Norway. Visit her website at www.constanceonilssen.com.

Akin Duzakin is a Turkish-Norwegian illustrator and children's author. He was nominated for the Astrid Lindgren Memorial Award in 2007 and 2008. He has collaborated with Constance Ørbeck-Nilssen on several books, including *Why Am I Here?* and *I'm Right Here* (both Eerdmans). Akin lives in Norway. Visit his website at www.akinduzakin.com.

Kari Dickson grew up bilingually, speaking both English and Norwegian. Her previously translated titles include *My Father's Arms Are a Boat* (Enchanted Lion), which was a 2014 Mildred L. Batchelder Honor Book. When she is not translating, she works as a tutor in Scandinavian studies at the University of Edinburgh.